Come away from the water, Shirley

John Burningham

Thomas Y. Crowell Company, New York

Copyright © 1977 by John Burningham. All rights reserved.
Printed in Italy.
ISBN 0-690-01360-4 0-690-01361-2 (LB)
CIP in back of book

Of course it's far too cold for swimming, Shirley

We are going to put our chairs up here

Why don't you go and play
with those children?

Mind you don't get any of that filthy tar
on your nice new shoes

Don't stroke that dog, Shirley,
you don't know where he's been

That's the third and last time I'm asking you whether you want a drink, Shirley

Careful where you're throwing those stones.
You might hit someone.

You won't bring any of that
smelly seaweed home, will you, Shirley

Your father might have a game with you
when he's had a little rest

We ought to be getting back soon

Good heavens! Just look at the time.
We are going to be late if we don't hurry.

Also by John Burningham:

THE BABY
THE BLANKET
THE CUPBOARD
THE DOG
THE FRIEND

THE RABBIT
THE SCHOOL
THE SNOW
MR. GUMPY'S MOTOR CAR

Library of Congress Cataloging in Publication Data

Burningham, John.
    Come away from the water, Shirley.

    SUMMARY: Shirley's adventures at the beach are
interspersed with familiar parental warnings.
    [1. Pirates—Fiction. 2. Fantasy] I. Title.
PZ7.B936Co3   [E]   77-483
ISBN 0-690-01360-4
ISBN 0-690-01361-2 (lib. bdg.)
Printed in Italy by A. Mondadori, Verona.